We Like...

"I like to cook," says Tiana.
"So do I!" says Naveen.

"I like music," says Naveen.
"So do I!" says Tiana.

"I like to dance," says Tiana.
"So do I!" says Naveen.

"I like to sing," says Naveen.
"So do I!" says Tiana.

"I like cake," says Tiana.
"So do I!" says Naveen.

"I like you," says Naveen.

"So do I!" says Tiana.